W9-BSG-142

JACQUELINE JULES art by MIGUEL BENÍTEZ

Albert Whitman & Company
Chicago, Illinois

Don't miss the first six **ZAPATO POWER** books!

Freddie Ramos Takes Off
Freddie Ramos Springs into Action
Freddie Ramos Zooms to the Rescue
Freddie Ramos Makes a Splash
Freddie Ramos Stomps the Snow
Freddie Ramos Rules New York

Library of Congress Cataloging-in-Publication data is on file with the publisher.

Pictures by Miguel Benítez
First published in the United States of America
in 2018 by Albert Whitman & Company
ISBN 978-0-8075-9500-8

Printed in the United States of America
10 9 8 7 6 5 4 3 2 1 BP 23 22 21 20 19 18

For more information about Albert Whitman & Company,
visit our website at www.albertwhitman.com.

With many thanks to Marta Camacho Stewart

Contents

1. Air and Space Museum

Everyone in my class had questions about the Air and Space Museum.

"Will they have moon rocks?" Maria bounced in her bus seat.

"And space suits?" Geraldo added.

"What about bathrooms?" Jason asked. "I want to see how an astronaut goes potty."

While the bus parked in front of a big building, our teacher, Mrs. Blaine, stood up to repeat the same field trip rules we'd heard five times back at Starwood Elementary. Then she pointed at Maria's mom, who had come along to help keep an eye on us.

"If you're not with me or Mrs. Santos, you are not where you're supposed to be. Understand?"

"We do!" Hamza jumped up from his seat. "Let's go!"

Mrs. Blaine laughed and waved us on. "I'm glad you're so excited."

As we rushed up the steps,

my feet tingled inside my superpowered purple sneakers. I wanted to zoom all over the museum with my Zapato Power. But I had to be careful about using my super speed. Mrs. Blaine had said to stay with the class OR ELSE. I wasn't sure what OR ELSE

meant, but Mrs. Blaine made it sound like something I did not want to find out.

"Look up, Freddie!" Geraldo shouted.

Airplanes were hanging over our heads. I stopped in my tracks like I was stuck to the floor. I'd never seen a museum like this.

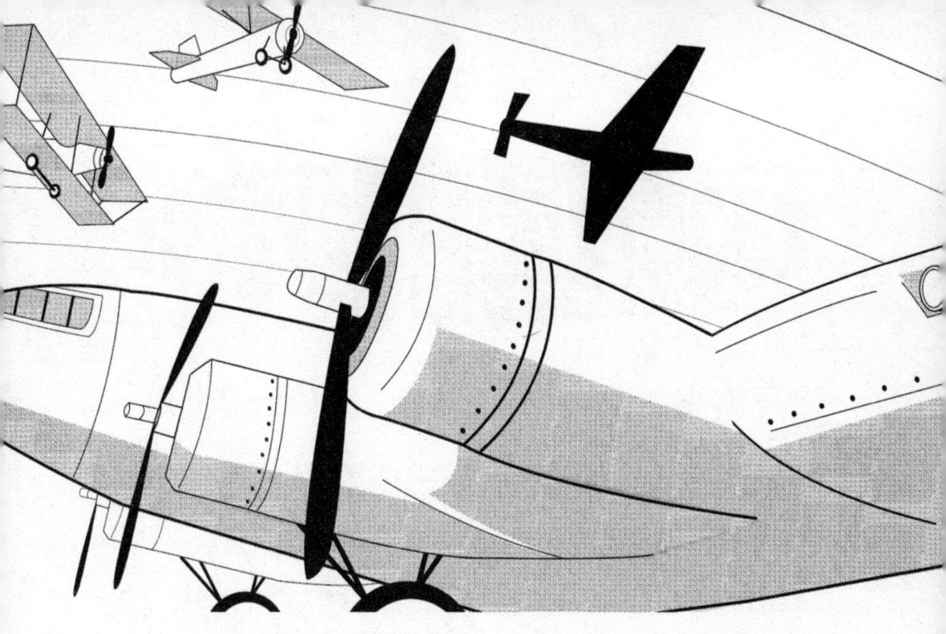

"Are you by yourself?" A security guard tapped me on the shoulder. "Children should always be in the company of an adult."

OOPS! My class was clear across the hall, standing around Mrs. Blaine and Mrs. Santos.

I touched a button on the purple wristband I always wear.

ZOOM! ZOOM! ZAPATO!

With my super zapatos, I could run ninety miles an hour in a cloud of invisible smoke. I could also jump really high and hear things from far away.

ZOOM! ZOOM! ZAPATO!

Mrs. Blaine had her finger out, counting heads. I snuck into the group just as she got to twenty-four, the number of kids in my class.

"Read the signs!" Mrs. Blaine

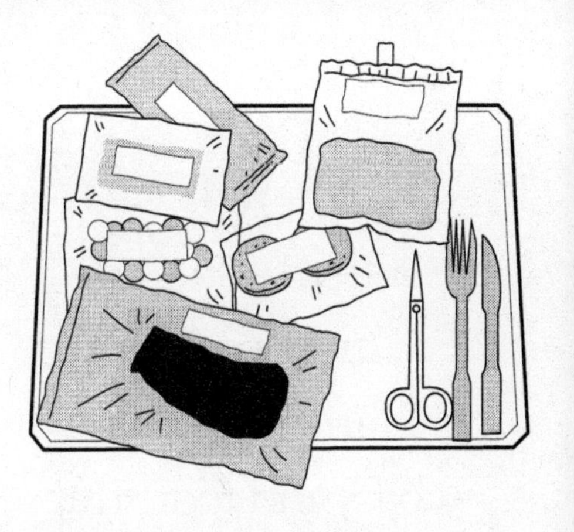

said as she led us into a room with space suits and space food and panels with dials. "Learn about the wonders of technology."

I thought about my friend Mr. Vaslov. He was a scientist who made inventions, including my superpowered sneakers. Mr. Vaslov would love seeing all these machines. I wondered if he had ever been here.

Then Jason started jumping up and down.

"There it is! A space toilet!" he called.

I went over with Geraldo and Maria to see. The space toilet had bars and foot straps. Astronauts had to wear seat belts to do their business.

"Eww!" Geraldo said.

Maria whistled. "It's big!"

Two guards with walkie-talkies and worried faces came into the room. That took my attention away from the space potty. Ever since I got my Zapato Power sneakers, I've tried to be a superhero. That means always

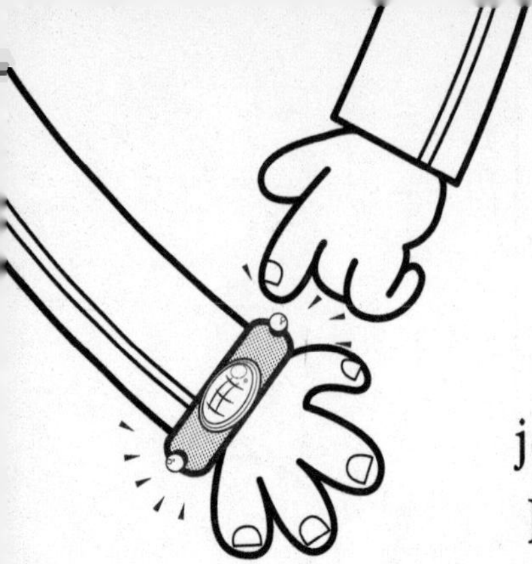

being on the lookout for hero jobs.

I rubbed the buttons on my wristband to turn on my super hearing.

"*We've scanned the floor,*" the taller guard said. "*No sign of the little boy.*"

"*It's been twenty minutes,*" the shorter one said. "*The mother is frantic.*"

A boy was lost in a big museum. He needed help. And I wanted to be a hero.

2. Secret Hero

Somebody little and lost would be crying. Could I hear it with Zapato Power? I moved closer to the doorway.

Sniff! Sniff! "Mommy!"

The sound was faint and almost drowned out by all kinds of other voices around me. But it was definitely there.

Sniff! Sniff! "Mommy!"

I checked behind me for Mrs. Blaine. She was with Jason at the space potty. Mrs. Santos was looking at some dials with Geraldo. No one would miss me if I was back in two blinks.

The next hall was gigantic, full of airplanes, rockets, and people. I darted in and out, hidden beneath my Zapato Power smoke.

ZOOM! ZOOM! ZAPATO!

I looked under airplane wheels, glass boxes with engine guts, and a billion signs I wished I had the time to read. No little boy. Where was he? I kept hearing him.

Sniff! Sniff! "Mommy!"

There were lots of families moving around, talking with each other. My Zapato Power caught it all.

"Don't pick your nose!"

"I wet my pants!"

"Can we have a snack?"

My ears hurt. In a big noisy place, my Zapato Power

hearing would be better turned off. But I had to find one sad voice calling for his mommy.

ZOOM! ZOOM! ZAPATO!

The cries led me to a small, dark room with a movie screen. At first, no one seemed to be in there. Then I heard sniffling again.

"*Mommy*."

A little boy in a red shirt and jeans was curled up like a snail, underneath a bench. No wonder the security guards couldn't find him.

"Come with me!" I told the little boy.

"NO! I want my mommy!"

The little boy wasn't making things easy, but I could still be a hero. All I had to do was get some help.

ZOOM! ZOOM! ZAPATO!

I dashed back to the space toilet room, expecting to find the security guards. They weren't there. Neither was my class. *Esto no era bueno*. Not good at all.

ZOOM! ZOOM! ZAPATO!

Back out in the big room, I spotted Mrs. Blaine counting heads beside a staircase leading up to the body of a giant airplane.

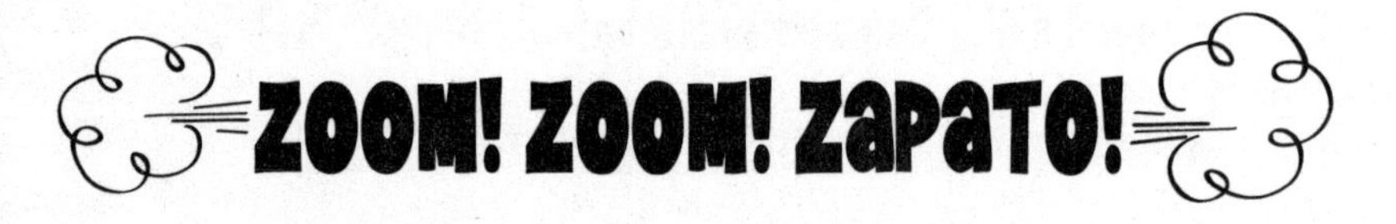

I made it just in time to be number twenty-four. But I couldn't stay in line. There was a lost little boy in the museum. And thanks to my super hearing, I was the only one who knew where he was.

ZOOM! ZOOM! ZAPATO!

Where were the security guards? Maybe I could see better from above. I pressed the button on my wristband for super bounce. YAY! I was up in the air next to all the airplanes hanging from the ceiling. It was great, except for almost bumping into a wing. To use my super bounce in a museum, I had to look both ways—up and down.

BOING! BOING! BOING!

Finally, I saw one of the guards

talking in a corner through his walkie-talkie.

I landed on the floor in a puff of smoke.

"Help!" I told the guard. "There's a little boy in a movie room, alone and scared."

"Where?"

I pointed, and the man ran with his walkie-talkie against his mouth.

"Child spotted! Bring mother!"

A few minutes later, the little boy was in his mom's arms. It made me feel good to see everybody crying happy tears, even though I had to watch from a distance. A superhero shouldn't stick close and take credit.

And a kid on a field trip shouldn't forget to stay with his class!

"Where's Freddie?"

With Zapato Power, I could hear Geraldo's voice somewhere behind me. But when I turned, I didn't see my friends. The big hall led to three smaller ones. Could I find my class before Mrs. Blaine started counting heads again?

ZOOM! ZOOM! ZAPATO!

3. The Gift Shop

The first hall had kids my size standing around a teacher. I rushed to join them until I realized it was a group from another elementary school. UGH!

The second hall had a school group too. Those kids were way too tall to be my age.

ZOOM! ZOOM! ZAPATO!

By the time I caught up with my class, my heart was pounding, but not from running. Mrs. Santos had noticed me.

"Freddie?" she questioned. "This is the first time I've seen you in a while. Have you been staying with the class?"

"I'm doing my best."

And I was. Except Zapato Power was distracting me. I heard people with problems I could solve.

"The baby's teddy bear dropped out of the stroller."

"Where's my bracelet? It was on my arm a minute ago!"

Instead of seeing how astronauts walked on the moon or the control panels in a cockpit, I was running around looking for a teddy bear and a bracelet. I pretty much missed everything until the end of the day when my class visited the gift shop. That's when I turned off my Zapato Power hearing to listen to my friends.

"Why is everything so expensive?" Jason whined. "I only have five dollars."

"I only have four," Geraldo said.

They were both doing better than I was. I had two dollars and thirty cents—all Mom had in her wallet that morning.

"Even the key chains cost too much," Maria complained.

Everything in the museum store was cool, from socks with moon pictures to kid-sized space suits.

Everybody, including me, wished they could buy at least one thing.

"Do you have something that costs less than two dollars?" I asked the white-haired man behind the cash register. His name tag said Bob, and he wore thick glasses and had stubble on his chin. He reminded me of my inventor friend, Mr. Vaslov.

"Follow me!" His friendly smile let me know I had asked the right person.

Bob led me to a spinning metal rack filled with postcards. They all had colorful pictures of astronauts, airplanes, and the moon.

"Seventy-five cents each," Bob said. "Four dollars for a pack of six."

¡Excelente! I called Geraldo over and soon my whole class crowded around. With so many happy kids grabbing, cards fell on the floor. That made a mess! But I didn't mind cleaning up while my friends paid for their postcards. It gave me extra time to pick one. Did I want the red airplane or the space walk?

While I tried to decide, everyone else followed Mrs. Blaine and Mrs. Santos out the door.

"Hey, kid!" Bob called to me. "Your class just left."

ZOOM! ZOOM! ZAPATO!

I raced out of the store in a panic. I'd missed my chance to get a souvenir. I couldn't miss the bus too.

"Sit with us, Freddie!" Maria waved. She was in the third row, beside Geraldo.

I plopped down at the end of the seat.

“So many airplanes!” Geraldo said. “They made me want to be a pilot.”

“I liked the room with the activities,” Maria said.

All around me, kids were talking about the stuff they’d seen at the museum. No one knew I'd been busy finding a lost little boy, a bracelet, and a teddy bear. No one knew how much I wanted to see what I'd missed. Sometimes being a superhero is lonely.

We got back to Starwood Elementary just before three o'clock. Mrs. Blaine looked tired, like counting heads all day was a big job. When the bell rang, she gave us a weak wave. No homework for the weekend!

ZOOM! ZOOM! ZAPATO!

In a blink I was out the back door of the school and up the stairs leading to Starwood Park Apartments. I should have been home two seconds later, feeding my guinea pig, Claude the Second. But just outside my apartment, 29G, my ears caught a moaning sound.

"*WAAAEEE! WAAAEEE!*"

I rubbed the buttons on my wristband to hear better.

"*WAAAEEE! WAAAEEE!*"

Did somebody else need help?

4. Creepy Storage Cellar

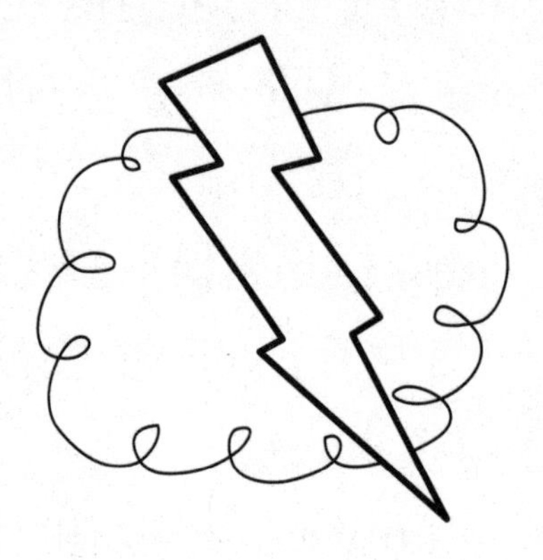

I followed the moaning sound down a set of concrete stairs outside Building G. At the bottom was the steel door to the basement storage room.

"*WAAAEEE! WAAAEEE!*"

What a strange cry! Who or what could it be? How could I find out? Only Mr. Vaslov had the keys to unlock the basement. Should I zoom around Starwood Park to look for him? If Mr. Vaslov wasn't in his toolshed inventing things, he was off in one of the apartments unclogging a drain or making a washing machine work. Even with super speed, it could take a while to find him. And I was worried that seconds might count. What if someone was hurt? For once, there was a quicker way than Zapato Power. I ran up the stairs to my apartment to use the telephone. Mom had posted Mr. Vaslov's phone number on the refrigerator.

"What's up, Freddie?" Mr. Vaslov sounded surprised. I'd never called him before. He knew running around was more my style.

"We have an emergency!" I hollered. "Someone is trapped in the Building G cellar."

"Be right there!"

Mr. Vaslov met me on the basement steps.

"Do you know who's trapped?" he asked as he opened the door.

It was dark inside the storage cellar. Our voices echoed while Mr. Vaslov reached along the wall to flip on the light.

"No," I admitted. "I just heard moaning."

"With your super hearing?" Mr. Vaslov questioned. "Or normal?"

"Both!" I answered.

The cellar had wire cages. Each one was filled with boxes and other things people didn't want in their apartments all year long. There were lots of Christmas trees—the kinds that aren't living. And one skeleton from Halloween. I was glad it was in a cage.

Everything was quiet. Really quiet. Not a single sound.

"Are you sure you heard

something, Freddie?" Mr. Vaslov asked.

I felt embarrassed, like I was letting him down. He always took me seriously, not like some grown-ups who think kids aren't important enough to listen to.

"Positive!"

We poked our noses against the wire holes and looked in the corners for something suspicious. *Nada*. Only piled up paint cans and spiderwebs.

"Nothing wrong here," Mr. Vaslov said finally. "This place is the same as this morning when I

put away some boxes for Mrs. Ramirez."

He looked at his watch. "Sorry, Freddie, I have to go."

Mr. Vaslov rushed out of the storage room and up the stairs. He didn't even stop to lock the door. I stood on the steps, watching him take off in a lopsided run. Why was he in such a hurry? Was someone waiting for him? I was curious. And when I get curious, I get an itch to use my Zapato Power.

ZOOM! ZOOM! ZAPATO!

With my super speed, it wasn't hard to get ahead to see where Mr. Vaslov was going. I hid behind a tree and watched him go up the walk into his own apartment at Starwood Park.

I snuck up to his doorstep to listen with my Zapato Power. As I rubbed the buttons on my wristband, I felt a little guilty. If

Mr. Vaslov hadn't told me why he was busy, maybe he didn't want me to know. Was I using my Zapato Power in the wrong way?

That's when I heard crying. A lot of crying. Someone inside Mr. Vaslov's apartment was upset. Who?

5. Snooping

"I'm scared."

The voice on the other side of the door was too high to be Mr. Vaslov's. It sounded young, like a kid.

"It will be all right. Don't worry," Mr. Vaslov answered.

Who was in Mr. Vaslov's apartment? What were they worrying about? Since I wasn't supposed to be snooping outside the door, I couldn't knock to ask questions no matter how much I wanted to. And it was getting dark. My mom would be coming home from work soon, expecting me to be doing my homework. Breaking the rules could mean no TV time.

ZOOM! ZOOM! ZAPATO!

I ran across Starwood Park, stopping short at the rail by the cellar steps. The moaning sound was back.

"*WAAAEEE! WAAAEEE!*"

What was making that noise? Was it the wind? Sometimes the wind sounds like someone moaning. But the air was perfectly still. The noise had to be someone crying.

"*WAAAEEE! WAAAEEE!*"

Mr. Vaslov forgot to lock the door. If I was brave enough, I could turn the knob and step inside.

"*WAAAEEE! WAAAEEE!*"

Superheroes are supposed to face danger, not run away. I forced myself to open the door and reach for the light switch. It was hard to find. Even worse, the concrete wall was cold and scratchy against the

palm of my hand. A cobweb broke across my face. Yucko!

As soon as I turned on the light, the crying stopped. The storage room was deathly still, just like last time. Should I poke around again? The skeleton in the cage seemed twice as big as before. Did it always have dark hollows for eyes?

I searched slowly, facing forward. I kept feeling like someone was behind me, reaching for my neck with long bony fingers.

"FREDDIE!" a voice shouted. "What are you doing down here?"

I whirled around. "Mom!"

Even though I knew she was mad, I was happy to see her. A little bit of yelling was better than being alone with a skeleton in a creepy storage room.

Mom grabbed me. "I came home from work and saw you weren't there. When I went back outside to look, I saw you walking down the cellar steps. *Yo estaba preocupada.*"

When Mom was worried, she hugged just as much as she yelled. I got squeezed a bunch before Mom was ready to hear my side of the story.

"I'm glad you care about others,"

she began, "and you always want to help."

Whew! Mom was seeing things my way! My TV time was safe.

"Checking the cellar is Mr. Vaslov's job, not yours, Freddie. I'm calling him right now."

Uh-oh! Would Mr. Vaslov tell Mom that he had just been here with me? I held my breath as I watched him walk up with his big set of keys. Luckily, Mr. Vaslov was more upset about his mistake than mine.

"I'm sorry," Mr. Vaslov told my mom. "This was my fault. The door should never have been left unlocked."

Mr. Vaslov jiggled the handle to make sure no one could get inside the cellar without him. Sometimes grown-ups don't have to tell you not to do something again. They make it impossible.

"Who is this?" Mom asked.

We all stopped thinking about the cellar to look at a boy standing a few feet away. He had dark hair and puffy red eyes.

"This is Alexis." Mr. Vaslov introduced us. "He's my great nephew."

"Nice to meet you," Mom said.

Alexis only nodded. His nose was just about as red as his eyes. Now I knew who had been crying behind Mr. Vaslov's door. I just didn't know why.

"How long are you visiting?" Mom asked.

"The weekend," Mr. Vaslov spoke for Alexis. "We're going to the Air and Space Museum tomorrow."

"Really?" I asked. "My class went there today on a field trip."

I stared at my shoes, thinking how my friends saw the museum while I was too busy with Zapato Power.

"There are lots of neat things there," I added.

"Would you like to go again,

Freddie?" Mr. Vaslov asked. "You could be our guide."

I looked at Mom. Having superpowers only changed some things. I still had to ask my mom before I could go anywhere.

"You are always so thoughtful!" Mom told Mr. Vaslov. "Freddie loves airplanes and spaceships."

¡Fantástico! I was getting a second chance to see the inside of a cockpit and everything else I'd missed.

What's more, I might get the chance to find out why Alexis had been crying.

Then there would be only one mystery left. Who was making noise in the cellar?

6. Back at the Museum

In the morning, Mr. Vaslov drove us to the museum. Alexis was a different person—all smiles and no sniffles. He talked on and on about making model airplanes with his dad.

"When we're finished, we hang them from my bedroom ceiling."

"I know." Mr. Vaslov nodded.

"That's why your father asked me to take you to the Air and Space Museum."

My dad was a soldier and a war hero. We never got a chance to make things together. I wondered if Alexis knew how lucky he was to have a dad in his life. Then I thought back to his crying and his puffy red eyes. His life wasn't perfect either.

"We're here!" Mr. Vaslov pulled open a glass door, and we moved into the gigantic hall with the airplanes overhead.

"Hey! Alexis!" I pointed. "Just like your bedroom at home."

"Not exactly." He laughed.

Mr. Vaslov was a lot more relaxed than Mrs. Blaine. No counting heads at all. He let Alexis read as many signs as he wanted without pushing him to hurry up. And he let me go inside the nose of a Boeing 747 twice.

In one of the rooms, Mr. Vaslov and I got interested in pictures of the space walks.

"Look at those huge backpacks," I said. "Are they engines? Do they make the astronauts fly?"

"They float, not fly," Mr. Vaslov explained. "There's oxygen in the packs to keep the astronauts alive."

"That makes sense," I said. "But a flying backpack sure would be awesome."

Mr. Vaslov winked. "I'll keep it in mind, Freddie."

Science museums are great places to get ideas for new inventions. Mr. Vaslov and I were so busy talking that we didn't notice Alexis wasn't nearby.

"WHERE IS HE?" Mr. Vaslov shouted. His eyes got as big as his round glasses.

"Don't worry!" I said. "I'm good at finding kids in this place."

ZOOM! ZOOM! ZAPATO!

¡No hay problema! I found Alexis in the next room, standing in front of something that looked to me like a ginormous kite.

"The Wright Brothers Flyer." He pointed. "The first plane! So cool!"

"It is!" Mr. Vaslov agreed, putting

his arms around Alexis in a bear hug.

Alexis was having too good a time to realize how much he had scared us. It was nice to see him smiling, but I still wondered why he'd been so unhappy the day before.

I got my chance to find out during lunch.

Mr. Vaslov bought us hamburgers, and we sat down in the table area with our trays.

"Drat!" Mr. Vaslov said. "I forgot to get napkins."

"I'll get them," I offered.

While I was over at the counter

pulling napkins from a metal box, Mr. Vaslov leaned his head toward Alexis. I could tell they were about to start a private conversation. All I had to do was rub the buttons on my wristband to listen in. Should I? It was really tempting. Too tempting! My fingers moved almost by themselves. Then my ears started hurting.

"*Don't feed your doll chocolate ice cream.*"

"*Gross! They put mustard on my sandwich!*"

"I don't like pickles!"

Blocking out the other people in the lunchroom and hearing Mr. Vaslov took all my concentration.

"I'm so happy the operation went well," he told Alexis. *"The doctor says your mom is recovering nicely."*

So that's what was wrong! Alexis was worried about his mom. If my mom had to have an operation, I'd be sad too.

I turned off my super hearing and went back to the table to eat my hamburger. Alexis and Mr. Vaslov stopped talking as soon as I sat down. That made me feel funny.

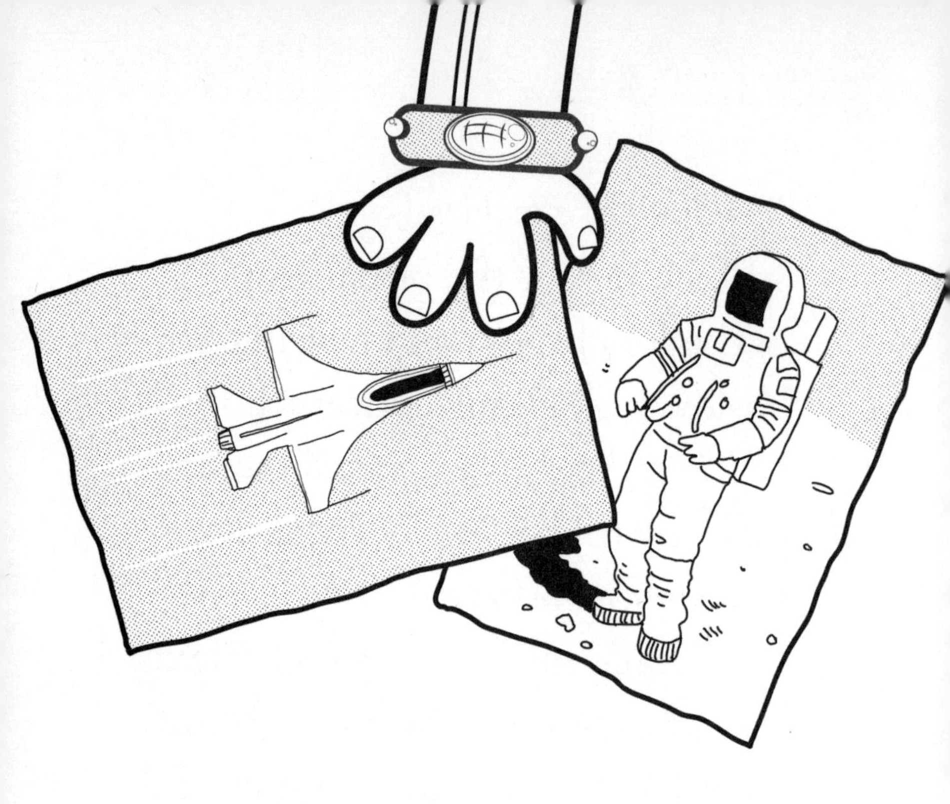

Later on, we went to the gift shop. I bought a postcard of a red airplane and one of the moonwalk showing astronauts wearing those fancy backpacks that looked like jet engines.

With Mr. Vaslov's help, Alexis picked out a model airplane covered in green and gold glitter. Alexis wanted it for his mom in the hospital. I knew that because I was eavesdropping from across the store.

"*Good choice*," Mr. Vaslov said. "*Your mom will love it.*"

As we left the museum, I kept wanting to say something to Alexis about his mom. But since I wasn't supposed to know she was in the hospital, I had to keep my mouth shut. Having superpowers is really complicated.

7. The Mystery Returns

"Want to hang out again tomorrow?" Alexis asked when we got back to Starwood Park.

"Sure!"

I couldn't wait to spend more time with Alexis. We'd had so much fun at the museum playing with all the dials and buttons.

As I walked back to my building,

I thought about things we could do together. Did Alexis play soccer? Did he like animals? Would he like my guinea pig, Claude the Second?

"WAAAEEE! WAAAEEE!"

Not again! I ran down the cellar steps and knocked on the basement door.

"Anybody there?" I called.

Just like last time and the time before, the crying stopped. And the door was locked tight. Mr. Vaslov had made sure of that. I had to go home and leave the mystery for another day.

***

In the morning, Alexis came over right after breakfast. The first thing we did was feed Claude the Second.

"Look at that!" Alexis was impressed. "He stands up and squeaks for his food!"

"Do you have a pet?"

"I keep asking." Alexis sighed.

"And Dad keeps saying, 'one day.' Maybe he'd let me get a guinea pig. It stays in a cage and doesn't run around like a cat."

"Is that what you want?"

"Yes," Alexis admitted. "I'd love a kitty."

When we were done playing with Claude the Second, Alexis looked out the window.

"It's sunny. Do you like soccer?" he asked.

I grabbed my ball, and Alexis grinned. He seemed just as happy as I was that we liked so many of the same things.

We went outside to the grassy area between buildings. Alexis played on a soccer team, and he knew practice drills. I didn't even think about turning on my super speed. Using Zapato Power for sports was like cheating.

We kicked the soccer ball for over an hour. Then we sat on the steps of the storage cellar to rest. Mom saw us through the window and brought us a snack.

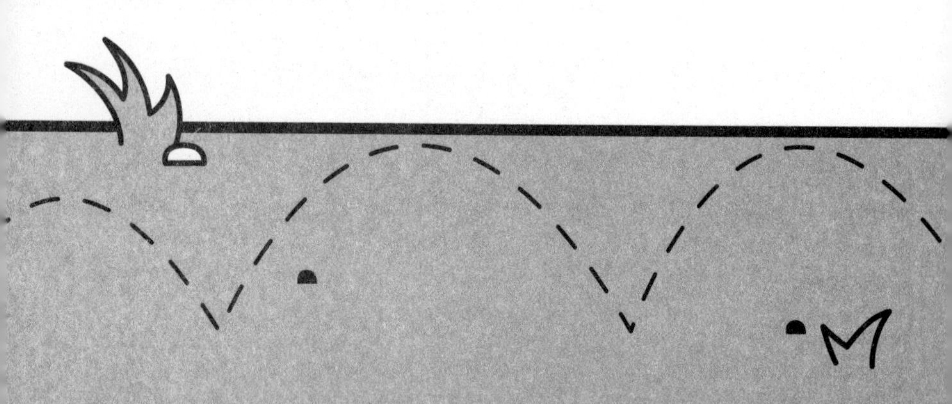

"This trip is turning out to be nice," Alexis said with his mouth full of cookies. "I thought I'd hate it."

"How come?" I asked.

Alexis hung his head. "My mom had an operation on Friday. My parents sent me here so my dad could spend more time at the hospital."

Suddenly I felt like a sneaky snoop. If I had just waited, Alexis

would have told me why he'd been crying on Friday. Now it was too late. I had to ask a question I already knew the answer to.

"Is your mom all right?"

Before Alexis could tell me, something got our attention.

"WAAAEEE! WAAAEEE!"

The crier in the storage cellar was back. Who or what was it?

"WAAAEEE! WAAAEEE!"

"It sounds like a hungry animal," Alexis said. "Once, our neighbor's cat got stuck under my house. It cried just like that."

If Alexis was right, this was an emergency! A job for a hero with super speed. ME!

"I'll get Mr. Vaslov to unlock the door!"

"And I'll get food," Alexis said.

He went in one direction, and I went in the other.

ZOOM! ZOOM! ZAPATO!

Hmm...Mr. Vaslov wasn't in his toolshed. Where should I look next? Maybe my Zapato Power hearing could help. I rubbed the buttons on my wristband and circled the buildings.

ZOOM! ZOOM! ZAPATO!

"Watch out for the dog poo!"

"Want to play jump rope?"

"If you don't share, I'm going to tell Mamá!"

At first, all I heard was kids playing outside. Then I followed a voice that sounded like Mrs. Ramirez in 20G. She was on her doorstep, crying out to our neighbor Mrs. Tran in 21G. Something was wrong!

I stepped around the corner, so I could hear without being seen. With Zapato Power, listening in on other people was too easy.

"*¡Mi gatita!*" Mrs. Ramirez sniffled. "*Where could she be?*"

"*Don't worry,*" Mrs. Tran said. "*We'll find your sweet kitty.*"

So Alexis was right. We did have

a hungry cat to rescue. If I could find Mr. Vaslov with the keys, I'd be a hero!

ZOOM! ZOOM! ZAPATO!

I ran around the buildings again. No sign of Mr. Vaslov. My super speed wasn't helping! I was ready to try a phone. Then I heard Alexis call my name.

"Freddie! Come look!"

Alexis was standing by the open cellar door, waving. Mr. Vaslov was beside him.

"We solved the mystery!"

8. Cat Trouble!

Mr. Vaslov had been in his apartment when Alexis went back for food. They rescued a little black cat before I had a chance to help.

"Now I know why we didn't see her before," Mr. Vaslov said. "Cats hide when they're frightened."

"So how did you find her this

time?" I asked.

There had to be a good reason why Alexis got to be the hero and not me.

"We gave her some leftover chicken," Alexis said. "Poor little thing was starving."

Alexis pointed at the kitten while she gobbled food. "Look! She doesn't have a collar. She must be a stray."

Mr. Vaslov nodded. "That might explain why she was stuck in the cellar by herself."

"She needs a home!" Alexis said. "I want to keep her!"

Yikes! The cat had to belong to Mrs. Ramirez. Alexis didn't know he was about to take somebody else's pet. This was the kind of thing a hero was supposed to stop. But Alexis was my friend. What was I going to do?

"Let's give the kitty a name." Alexis leaned down to stroke the cat. "Do you have any ideas, Freddie?"

A name? Alexis was getting attached. If I didn't act fast, he'd be crushed when he found out the truth. How could I explain? Alexis didn't know I had super hearing, and Mr. Vaslov didn't know I had been snooping.

Then I thought about Mrs. Ramirez crying at 20G. Sometimes you go for the problem you can solve and leave the rest for later.

I scooped the cat up in my arms.

ZOOM! ZOOM! ZAPATO!

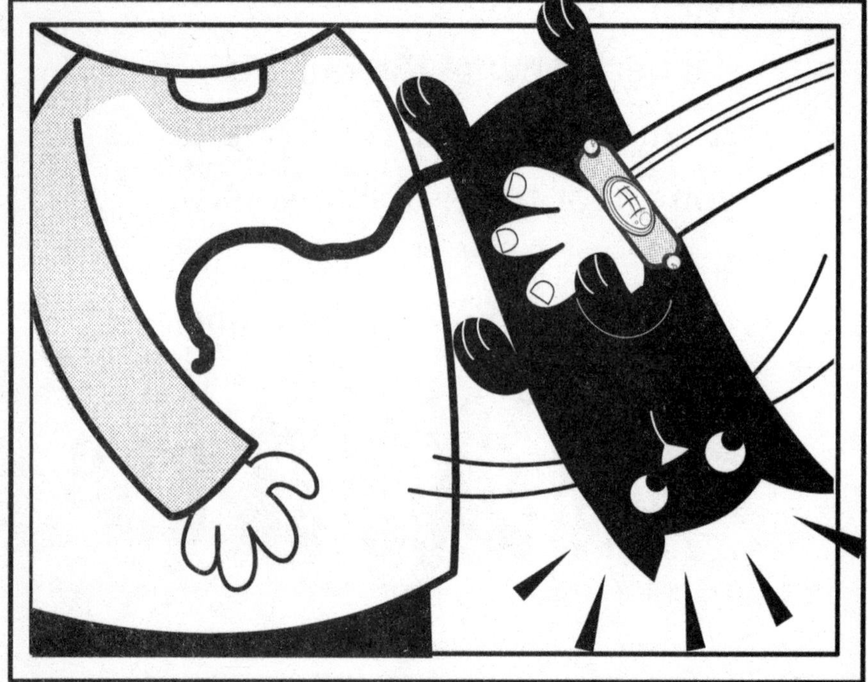

NO!

"Freddie!" Mr. Vaslov called after me. "WHERE ARE YOU GOING?"

ZOOM! ZOOM! ZAPATO!

I raced around the corner with the little black cat, ready to hear Mrs. Ramirez thanking me, telling me I was a hero.

Except when I got there, I saw Mrs. Ramirez hugging another cat. And it wasn't a little black kitten like the one in my arms. That cat was gigantic, with white fur sticking out all over and a don't-mess-with-me face.

"See," Mrs. Tran soothed. "I told you we'd find her."

"MEOW!"

The black kitty cried and squirmed in my arms. She didn't seem to like me much.

At that moment, I didn't like me too much either.

Mr. Vaslov came running up. Alexis was right behind him.

"Sorry!" I cried. "I made a mistake!"

The black cat wiggled down to the ground. "Meow!" She ran away.

Mr. Vaslov put a firm hand on

my shoulder. "Let Alexis get the kitty. We should talk."

It was time to admit I'd messed up. Not just with the cat but the field trip too.

"My super hearing gets me into trouble. I'm using it too much!"

Mr. Vaslov rubbed his stubbly chin, listening quietly. "I see."

Some grown-ups make it easy. They tell kids what to do. Mr. Vaslov made me figure things out on my own. Not so easy.

"I can't control myself!" I added.

"Are you sure?" Mr. Vaslov raised his bushy eyebrows.

That was a good question. I didn't use super speed when I played sports with my friends.

"Not really." I scratched my head. "Maybe I could wait till I'm sure super hearing will solve a problem, not make one."

"Good plan, Freddie." Mr. Vaslov smiled.

Just then, Alexis came back. "The kitty's hiding again! Can you hear her?"

Mr. Vaslov turned to me with a wink. "I can't, but maybe Freddie can."

The cat wasn't crying anymore. My super hearing wasn't helping. Running all over Starwood Park didn't work either. Finally, brainpower helped me figure it out.

"Of course!" Alexis agreed. "She's hungry!"

The kitty was by the cellar door, finishing her food.

"You should call her Star," I told Alexis, "for Starwood Park."

"Perfect!" he said. "It will remind me how I found her here with you!"